MY SEXPERIENCE
(Tales of a college Playboy).

Pierce Clark

TABLE OF CONTENT.

Chapter 1: I CAME TO HELP

My name is Jack, I am what a high school girl would call dreamy, intelligent,nice haircut, six feet tall, nice smile, broad muscular chest, chiseled abs and chin, a cute innocent but guilty face and my most prized possession, my 7 and half inch tool. So, these attributes gave me confidence, eloquence, and I find both younger girls and older girls around me. And of course being the ladies man that I am, I don't need to say much before I get a hot girl on my bed screaming harder from the influence of my good strokes and thrusts. Aside from my looks and physique, there's something else about me that attracts the ladies that I can't really understand. Guess nature calls them pheromones . Most times, I wonder how I manage to still have very good grades despite all these, well, I know it's because I always find time to study. My guys know about all these and usually comes to me for some tips on sexual issues, hence they gave me the name sex-DEMIGOD or just "the demi".

I live alone with my mother, who is a workaholic, but I don't really care because I have school to keep me company. My mother filed a divorce with my dad when I was a kid because of domestic violence , he was always hitting her, such a weakling he was hitting a lady.

Mandy is the mother of two little boys and also, my mother's best friend. They have been that way since I can remember, seeing them for the first time, one will believe they are sisters. from my POV, Mandy is 5 foot 7, and it's hard to tell she's a mother aside from the little extra fat a mother gets from pregnancy and childbirth, she has beautiful green eyes and overall, she is a beautiful lady. She usually comes to visit us, and my mother and I also go to visit her, during those times she would share how she has been sexually frustrated since her husband passed. I usually alternate between calling her aunt and her name even though we aren't related.

So, it's now summer. I was really bored staying at home all by myself cus my mother is usually very busy during this time. Due to the constant complaint I was giving my mom about how bored I was at home, she brought up the idea that I should go to Mandy's for the weekend cus she(Mandy) was grieving her husband. After all the packing and transportation, I was in Brooklyn by 6pm on Friday, the same day my mother and Mandy, my aunt, will attend a gala together. When I arrived, I only saw Mandy, guess her kids had gone to their friend's place. Mandy was getting ready to attend a gala. This was her first major outing since her husband James had passed... during COVID... although from a heart attack, not COVID... like everyone assumed. Since she rarely went to any social event recently, she was going out with my mother, who said she had to get back out there(into the world cus, she was always indoors, in her shell)... at only 44, she had to move on... James would want her to, my mother would say.

Mandy bought herself a new red dress that showcased her firm tits and great ass... having stayed in amazing shape, and had even lost the last of her baby-carrying weight (which she'd held onto for almost twenty years) during the two years the world had shut down.

Bowing to my mother's influence, she'd even bought some new lingerie... My mother frequently urged her to always be ready just in case she ended up in a promising situation. Truth be told, Mandy wasn't sure she was ready to get back out there, nor was she expecting to hook up with anyone tonight or in the near future, but she did enjoy dressing up... James had always loved seeing her in sexy lingerie... garter-belts and stockings really driving me wild... A sexy lingerie underneath her short, sexy (but sophisticated) dress was a bit of a rush. She felt particularly naughty when she decided to go extra, and she reminded herself she'd need to be careful not to inadvertently present any X-rated displays.

Mandy put on the garter-belt and carefully slid the silky sheer mocha stockings with the sexy seams down the back (James had loved the seams as well as the Cuban heels), and examined herself in the mirror. She had to admit she looked pretty amazing! Her 34B tits were still firm. Her trim figure was back to her early twenties, and her legs looked amazing in the dark mocha shade... her favourite shade, since it was as close as she ever came to showing off a good tan, since she burned so damn easy... the only drawback of being a redhead.

She examined her ring finger. Particularly her ring... her wedding ring. Which she hadn't removed since her husband's tragic passing. She stared at it for a full minute, perhaps two, before she slowly and ceremoniously removed it.

But it slipped past her fingers, ricocheted off the linoleum floor, and rolled under her bed.

Mandy sighed. "Fuck!"

She got down on the floor and crawled under her bed, reaching for the ring. Luckily it was just within her reach. She clutched it between her fingers and slowly pulled her hand back.

Once she could reach it with both hands, she slid it back onto her finger, taking this misstep as a sign that she shouldn't stop wearing it yet, and went to continue backwards from under the bed. But then she realised she was stuck. Her pearl necklace, the last gift James had ever given her, had caught on something in the bedsprings. it was very special to her, so no way did she want to damage it!

She cursed rather loudly, "Mother fucker!"

i was just down the hallway in my bedroom when i heard my Aunt curse, and it was an odd curse, since i would love to become a literal "mother fucker". .my Aunt was my number one stroke fantasy... in my opinion she'd always been hot, but she'd become amazingly so since the outbreak of COViD. Her habitually wearing nylons every day added fuel to my number one fetish.

I went silently down the hall to my Aunt's room, the door slightly ajar, and peeked inside. My eyes went wide when I saw the last thing I could have expected... My Aunt's amazing ass was bent over, with her pussy (and red landing strip) within full view.

Mandy sighed. i was home, and secretly watching through the keyhole, but she didn't want to call out to me, since i would then arrive to find her in a very awkward (and exposed!) position. Yet she couldn't just remain there partway under her bed all night!

I pulled out my phone and opened the door as I quietly tiptoed into my Aunt's room. I knew it was wrong, but couldn't resist. I snapped a couple pictures from just inside the doorway.

My cock hardened in a heartbeat, and I must quietly pull down my swimming trunks (which was all I was wearing, since I'd just come out of the backyard pool), and so here I was, gloriously naked (but not afraid) inside my Aunt's bedroom.

I still knew it was wrong... so damn wrong... but regardless, I shifted the camera to video and began filming as I slowly stroked my cock.

Mandy knew it would be terribly embarrassing, but she had no other choice, so she called out, "jackie!"

I kept silently and slowly stroking my cock as I admired my Aunt's ass... my Aunt's pussy... and the mocha soles of my Aunt's stocking-clad feet.

Mandy, becoming very impatient, tried to wriggle herself out ever so cautiously... wiggling her ass... twisting her body back and forth... unaware that she was putting on a terrific show for a nineteen-year-old college boy, me.

"Jesus," I whispered to myself, as my Aunt flexed her ass around in a sensual way.

"Fuck, fuck, fuck!" Mandy cursed, still stuck.

I admired the sexy seams up the back of her legs, took a deep breath, snuck out of the room and called back in from the hallway, "Are you okay, Aunt?"

"Thank God," Mandy muttered to herself.

"Oh my," I said, acting surprised as I entered the room. "Oh dear, you're not okay, are you, Aunt?"

"Jack, I'm stuck," she said, humiliated to be caught half naked by me, and frustrated at being stuck.

"Oh," I said, as I moved closer, moving a little closer as I kept filming my Aunt...my eyes moving from her ass to the soles of her feet, to her pussy... her mostly shaved pussy... to her entire perfect pose.

"Help me call your mother," Mandy said.

"Okay," I said, but actually I got right behind my Aunt, then knelt down to film a closeup of her amazing ass and her even-better-than-shaved pussy.

"Hurry," Mandy urged, mortified to be stuck in such a predicament.

"Okay," I said as I bent down to admire my Aunt's pussy from just inches away, instead of calling my mother like I said I'd do. i Set My phone on its side to continue filming.

To Mandy it must have sounded like my voice was much closer to her now... and then must have felt a hot little breath on her thigh. Her eyes went wide(I guess from the little gasp I heard). As it dawned on her that I was crouching right behind her so I could actually grind her ass. "Jack?" She called my name tentatively.

i froze.i Knew i'd probably out myself if I didn't answer, but I was so transfixed by this view of my Aunt's ass and pussy that I couldn't speak.

"Jack?" she repeated.

"Yes?" I asked, carefully advancing my hands along the floor as I inched even closer to her pussy.

"What are you doing?"

"Your pussy is so pretty," I crooned dreamily,my lips and tongue now only a couple of inches away from it, as I had changed my position with my back to the ground.

"Jack, I can feel your breath on my privates! So stop whatever you're doing, and phone your mother so she can come and rescue me," Mandy ordered sternly. But unfortunately, feeling my breath on her pussy was making her tremble ever so slightly. So if she ignored the moral issues being compromised here... which she definitely mustn't do...my grossly inappropriate attentions weren't totally bad.

"Aunt, I can't resist you," I said as I pondered what to do next.

I could lick her pussy...I fucking loved eating pussy... There was one time,my neighbor had a daughter who was 18 years old. I'd frequently eat her pussy and she was always appreciative, which usually led her to doing things for me she wouldn't do for any other guys. I had just finished my first year of college, and although I'd fucked a few High school Seniors ,I preferred older women. So far I'd fucked two professors and a couple dozen MiLFs, including the executive assistant to the Dean, a sexy Mexican janitor, and the owner of my favourite restaurant, a hot Afghan woman. These are stories for another day.

But now I had the chance to slide my cock into my ultimate dream MiLF...my very own Aunt! The idea of fucking her had long been my ultimate turn-on and my most compelling stroke fantasy.

"Jack, let's try another approach. I just need you to slide under the bed and unhook my necklace from wherever it's stuck," Mandy instructed, trying to get me to focus on her problem... even as she continued to feel my hot breath on her pussy... making her shiver... which confused her.

"Aunt, your pussy's getting wet," I said, and I couldn't resist leaning forward and licking the wetness.

"Jack, what are you doing?" Mandy squealed when she felt my tongue on her pussy.

"Just relax, Aunt," I said, knowingly I had a gifted tongue that usually had women moaning with pleasure in almost no time... in my senior year of high school my class teacher Barbara... had taught me all about the ways to pleasure a woman... when she took my virginity two days after I turned eighteen.

"Jack, stop that right now," Mandy demanded as my tongue parted her pussy lips.

"You taste so good," I said, knowing that complimenting the taste of a woman's pussy made her more comfortable... although this was an entirely new level of kink... being my Aunt and all. That said,I wasn't lying... she did taste good... very, very good.

"Jack, what you're doing is wrong," Mandy said even though her body was betraying her, since my tongue felt so good... it was almost two years since her pussy had been touched by a man... by someone's tongue... her husband had been a great pussy licker(from what I hear by eavesdropping on her and my mother's conversation) , and it seems I have a better skill as she was moaning sensually.

"Does it feel wrong?" I asked as I probed her pussy hole.

"Jackieee," she moaned, unable to complete a sentence with my tongue really working her long-neglected pussy over... she'd masturbated exactly twice in the past two years... coming only once... giving up the other time when she couldn't get herself off from what she told my mother.

"Just relax, Aunt," I said confidently, since my Aunt's voice wasn't angry or furious, but confused and morally righteous.

"You need to stooooooop," my Aunt Demanded, although she added a loud moan when she felt my finger begin tapping on her clit while I probed her pussy.

"I can't, Aunt, " I said. "I've fantasised about doing this forever."

"You have?" Mandy asked, so confused. She knew this was wrong... yet i was right... it felt so good. Learning that I had fantasised about her was completely shocking... although she knew I appreciated her ass... having noticed me staring at them on multiple occasions, those asses were really shapy and big, soft even, they'll jiggle as she walks, and I can't get enough of the view.

"Every day," I said as I tapped her clit and licked her pussy.

"But you're my friend's son," Mandy moaned, pointing out the obvious... even as an orgasm rose inside her.

"I know, but it doesn't matter, we aren't even related," i said as I
really worked my Aunt over... sensing she was close to coming from my aggressive tongue and my finger tapping on her clit, I increased the tempo of my motion.

"Oh God, jackkieeee," Mandy moaned, knowing this was so wrong, yet unable to deny the pleasure I was giving her.

"Cumm for me, Mandy,"i said, using the sexy, naughty term i'd used in so many of my sexcapades, as I slid two fingers inside my Aunt's very wet pussy, and although I usually ate a woman while she was on her back and the g-spot was easy to find,i probed my fingers around for a moment until I found her g-spot, and she climaxed almost instantly.

"Oh jackiieeeeee!!" Mandy screamed as her orgasm hit her, and she trembled violently.

He felt her juices flooding my hand, so I quickly pulled my fingers out and lapped up my Aunt's sweet cum.

Mandy couldn't believe the intensity of her orgasm... as her body endured wave after wave of euphoria... briefly forgetting it was her best friend's son who'd gotten her off.

I was in my own rapture, thinking with the left part of my brain, and after long moments of savouring my Aunt's sweet nectar, scooted up, and without even a second thought,I slipped my seven-inch dick into my Aunt's leaking pussy.

"Jackkieeee," Mandy moaned in weak protest as she felt my cock...my very big cock... slide into her pussy.

"i have to, Mandy," i groaned as i started fucking my Aunt.

"Oh God, Jack," Mandy moaned, as pleasure consumed her... her first orgasm has not even completely faded away as a second one began rising inside her.

"Your pussy feels so good,Aunt," i said, as I pumped in and out of her... in awe that at long last I was fucking my Aunt!

"You shouldn't be fucking your Aunt," Mandy moaned, turned on not only from my dick inside her, but the 'partially incestuous' wordplay...

"I know,Aunt, " I said. "But do you want me to stop?"

Here was Mandy's chance to halt this incestuous act, yet now she didn't want it to end. She wanted me to keep right on fucking her... so... she replied with great eagerness, "No jack, keep fucking Aunt. Give Aunt all of that big dick!"

"Oh yeah," i said, in awe that my Aunt was now enthusiastically agreeing to commit a kind of incest. I began fucking her faster... harder....

"Oh yeah, fuck your Aunt , baby, fuck your Aunt 's pussy," Mandy moaned. Take this big dick mandy, take all of my cock, I said.I always talk nasty in the heat of the moment... But never quite like this, guess I have really fantasized this moment.

I was in complete rapture as I did what my Aunt wanted... slamming into her from behind... but wishing I could see her face while I fucked her. There was just something so sexy about a woman's expressions while she was getting fucked.

As I fucked her hard, she suddenly noticed her necklace was no longer caught on the bed. Wanting to get into a different position, her back not fond of this position, she said,

"I'm not stuck anymore. Help me out of here."

"Okay," I said, hoping this interruption wouldn't extinguish the lustful fire between us . I pulled out, and while admiring her ass,I lifted up the bed frame.

Mandy rolled out from under it.

I slowly lowered the bed back down.

Mandy saw my dick for the first time...my magnificent dick... glistening with her wetness... and she just had to taste it. She stepped close to me and asked, overwhelmed with lust, "is it okay if Aunt sucks your big dick?"

"Okay? it's more than okay,"I replied, and my Aunt's lips were wrapped around my dick before finished speaking.

I always found that older women gave better blow jobs, and that assessment was proven indisputably correct as my beautiful Aunt bobbed on my dick with smooth precision... and to her credit, she took all seven and half inches in her mouth...

My tool was almost the same size as her husband's only bigger, so she could passionately deep throat it... for thankfully sucking dick isn't a skill you lose after two years of not practising. She'd always loved sucking cock... in college she'd been well-known for her cock sucking skill. Truth was, she loved controlling a man's orgasm, and right now, although she wanted my dick back in her pussy... she was also craving my load... since cum was something else she'd sorely missed for the last two years.

"Oh fuck, mandyyy," i groaned, as she expertly worked on my dick, and I watched her do it... looking so fucking hot with my dick all the way down her throat.

"MMmmmmm," she purred, wanting me to know how much she was enjoying my dick.

i knew i wouldn't last long, this blow job from my aunt was too intense for me to control my boiling balls, and I warned, "Aunt, i'm going to come real soon!"

Mandy pulled back from my dick just long enough to say, "Then come! I want your load in my mouth, jackie," before she resumed sucking with even more hunger and lust.

"Oh fuck, Mandyyy," i groaned, knowing I was about to erupt.

Mandy sucked on my cock with reckless abandon for another fifteen seconds, before she heard me grunt, felt my cock twitch in her mouth, and then the warm, creamy load erupted into her mouth, surged flavourful across her taste buds, and glided smoothly down her throat.

"Oh Aunt,"I groaned,my entire body trembling as I came in my Aunt's mouth... rope after rope shooting into her.

Mandy kept bobbing until every drop of my sweet seed was in her belly before backing off, standing up and kissing me... messily... and passionately.

I kissed my Aunt back, and we spent two or three minutes engaged in the lustful passionate kiss.

Mandy needs my dick inside her, her pussy still on fire, broke the kiss and said, "i hope you reload quickly.Aunt needs to get fucked right now."

"Oh, I'm ready right now," I said, able to reload two or three times without a break.

"Then help me out of this dress and bra... I assume you'd like me to keep the stockings?" She said,

He agreed enthusiastically while I unzipped her dress.

Then once she was effectively naked, she resumcd speaking. "Now come to bed and fuck Aunt," taking me by the hand and leading me to her bed... the bed where she used to have sex with her husband.

I followed, and as my Aunt climbed onto her bed and onto her back,I knelt between her legs and admired her body.

"What are you waiting for?" Mandy asked, expecting me to fuck her right away.

"I'm just admiring your incredible beauty,"I said.

"Oh my Jackie," she said as she brought her left foot tomy chest and slid her nylon-clad sole up and down. "That's so sweet!"

"I mean it, Aunt,"I said. "You're the most beautiful woman I know."

She grasped my hard dick with the soles of her feet and smoothly stroked it, saying, "I'm also very flexible."

"That feels amazing."

"My husband loved my nylon foot jobs."

"Along with your big cock," she smiled as she gave me a nylon foot job.

"God, I can't believe we're really doing this."

"You didn't seem very surprised when you licked my pussy and fucked me under the bed."

"I can't believe I did that either,"I said. "it was a huge risk... and it could have gone a lot differently than it did."

"I can't believe you took advantage ofAunt like that either," the Auntsaid, although she was obviously pleased with the end result.

"You didn't put up much of a fight," I pointed out.

"How could i?" My Aunt asked. "I was literally stuck and helpless."

"You're not stuck or helpless now," I smiled.

"No, I'm certainly not, you hot stud," she agreed, and she wrapped her legs around my waist and pulled me closer to her. "What i am now is horny, and i need you to fuck me. Think you can fuck your Aunt again right now?"

"I'm sure I can," I said, andiwas suddenly on top of my Aunt.

"Then fuck me," she said, wrapping her nylon-clad legs around me, and i slid inside her wet pussy.

"Okay,"I agreed, suddenly deep inside my Aunt.

"Oh fuck," Mandy moaned, "you feel so good inside Aunt." Mandy asked

"So hot," I said as I rested deep inside her.

"Now fuck me, jack. fuck your Aunt ," Mandy said, looking into my eyes.

"Okay,"I nodded, as I began slowly fucking her while staring into her green eyes.

"Oh yes, baby, that feels so good," she moaned.

He leaned down and kissed her as I fucked her... her legs still wrapped around me ... the fucking slow and passionately. Mandy slid her tongue in my mouth, and I responded by reciprocating... while I slowly fucked her... or more accurately... made love to her.

For three... four... five minutes... we kissed.

We French kissed.

We slowly made love.

But then Mandy needed it faster... harder. She broke the kiss and said, looking into my eyes, and said as she spread her legs wide, "Fuck me, jack. Fuck Aunt hard."

"Oh Aunt,"i said as I cupped her firm tits and began fucking her faster.

"Oh, yes boy, fuck your Aunt , fuck your Aunt with that big cock," Mandy moaned.

"You like this,Aunt?" i asked, loving how completely she was into the incest aspect.

"Oh yes, jackkie," Mandy moaned. "Aunty loves being fucked by you, jackkie."

"Then this is my pussy from now on," I said as I grabbed her legs, pulled them together, and began to pile drive my aunt... This angle allows me to drill deep and make my woman go wild.

"Yes, baby," Mandy agreed mindlessly, "you can have Aunt's pussy whenever you want it."

"That will be often," I assured her, in awe that this would be more than just a one-time thing.

"It'd better be," Mandy moaned, loving how deep my dick was going into her and the way I was taking control.

"Oh, that's a promise,"I assured her as I really began to pound my Aunt.

"Oh yes, get that dick deep insideAunt," Mandy moaned loudly, her second orgasm rising quickly.

I was really giving it to my Aunt... and this position always led to an epic climax for my women..

"Oh, i love your big fucking cock insideAunt," Mandy declared as she began bucking her ass up to try and get my cock even deeper.

"Come for me,Aunt," I ordered. "Come all over my cock."

"Oh yes, harder, harder, harder," Mandy demanded, so close to coming.

A dozen more strokes, and Mandy screamed as her newest orgasm hit, "Yes, you mother fucker."

As my Aunt's orgasm hit,i kept fucking her,my own second orgasm rising.

"Jesus," Mandy moaned weakly as she collapsed on the bed, her body on fire, as wave after wave of pleasure coursed through her.

"You look so hot," I said, loving the vulnerability of this woman as she came.

"You too," she said, as she enjoyed the orgasm.

A couple dozen strokes later as I was about to come again,I said, "I'm about to come again."

"Come inside your Aunt, honey," she said, wrapping her legs around me and pulling me close.

"Okay,"I said, and I almost immediately did just that... shooting my load into my Aunt.

"Oh yes, fill your Aunt," she moaned, loving the feeling of my cum shooting into her pussy.

"Fuck,"i grunted.

Once I was done,I rolled off of her and collapsed.

For a couple minutes as we both recovered, there was only silence.

That was eventually interrupted when Mandy's phone rang. She looked at the clock and said, "Shit, I'm late."

"For what?"

"The gala," she said, getting out of bed and answering her phone. "I'm on my way."

'You haven't left yet?" my mother demanded.

"I am right now," she lied, as she grabbed her bra.

She hung up, and I said, "No panties, whenever I come to visit. That's a new rule."

"I can do that." She said,

"Perfect,"I said, "I'll be a Greek god with my entire stud body, and waiting for you when you get home later today."

"I can't wait," she said, already looking forward to the next round.

Chapter 2 : GAIN IN THE PLANE

It was holiday again, arggg I groaned to myself as the flight took off. It's gonna be a terrible holiday for me. I schooled in Havard, quite far from my mother's house in NY, that gave me the amount of freedom I needed to live my school life to the fullest. I went to parties and clubs, and still got one of the best grades of my schools first year students.

While in the plane, I couldn't help but reminiscence on all the sexcapades I had in schools with my lecturer, and the sexiest girl in my class and also the last time I went home and I smiled but the smile quickly ended as I remembered that Mandy and mom's best friend and one of my MILF partners has moved to Los Angeles.Mandy told me on text that she found a rich guy that's willing to take care of her and her kids and he wants them to come over and stay in his house over there.

While deep in thought, someone came by my side, and asked if I needed anything, she had to call twice before I snapped back to reality. There before my very eyes, the hostess , she was pretty and slim but there's something unique about her body, she's slim alright, but her hips are broad, I just couldn't help but notice. "And with such hips came incredibly big ass" I thought. After snapping to reality, I answered, "I don't need anything at the moment but it seems I'll definitely need something later" I said with a smile. She reciprocated my smile with a giggle, which I find really interesting. After she was done asking, she had to go to the other seats in front of me giving me a nice view of her ass, and I wasn't wrong because, She had a very nice backside view and a nice shape too coupled with a huge ass. I was sad initially, but that view seemed to have elated my mood and I said to myself

" how bout a little sexcapade on the plane, that won't be bad". Whenever the lady is passing by, she'll always look towards my direction and smile seductively. I don't know if she was actually trying to be seductive or actually doing her job and being nice, so I decided to find out. I signalled her to come over , without having anything particular to ask her. When she came, I immediately "asked if the restroom was free" and she said she thinks so but she would check right away and I followed her. I was a little disappointed in myself cuz I couldn't find something sensible to ask, but nonetheless, my rubbish question is gonna take us to a quiet private place, the restroom, and I'm gonna have my chance , I thought. When we got there, she checked to restroom and told me it was all empty that I could carry on with my business and headed for the door, as she was about leaving, I held her hand, and gently brought her back and I told her that I just wanted both of us to be alone that's why I asked the question. She was a little surprised but had the courage to ask me why I wanted to be alone with her, and I answered that I just wanna appreciate her beauty and tell her her beautiful and sexy she is (I used the word sexy so I'll know if she gets angry when addressed in a sensual manner). As I expected, she was blushing and grinning to my complement she said she usually receives compliments from guys older than her, not younger (calculation her age from my intuition, she's in her late 20s from 26-30). That's a good sign I smiled. She also complimented my looks and physique (which is quite usual for me). Then I went a step further and asked if she would mind me appreciating her beauty with a little peck and immediately, he smiled because soft laughter's and she said to me "Ok, I don't mind, but not on the lips though, my boyfriend would be pissed" she said laughing. So , I held her waist and pulled her closer and kissed her neck passionately. She couldn't help but grab my neck and a soft moan escaped her lips. With my other hand, I grabbed her ass, and to my surprise, they are one of the softest asses I have ever held. Then we both went inside the main restroom and I kissed her lips and neck passionately while unzipping her skimpy and fitted gown. I got halfway undressing her, just enough to expose her boobs and as I began sucking and fumbling, she was squeaking under my touch and her moan was getting louder, someone on the other segment of the restroom could actually hear us but we didn't care. I felt that the passengers would be looking for her now for her assistance, but she was exactly where I wanted her to be , with her boobs in my mouth. So after kissing and fumbling for a while, I took my hands down , over to her pubis, and I gently tapped her pussy through her panties and immediately she gave out a loud gasp. Her panties were so wet, we had to take them off, so it wouldn't obstruct my next line of action . After taking off the panties, I tapped on her bare pussy, her body trembling with every tap, and next

I proceeded to caress her clit region. She was moaning kinda loud at this point. I had to mute her with a kiss from time to time. All these times, she was leaning on the sink, so I carried her to sit on the sink, so I'll have full access, and after that I began fingering her, damn her pussy was so wet. I began with one finger, then two, then three and she couldn't help it, "mmhmm uh yes right there mmmm yeah" was all she could say,she was in ecstasy she would moan and hold my head as I continued fingering . When I found her g-spot, it was over, she couldn't hold it anymore, he gasped in three statements, she said " I am cummiinngg" and immediately he body went into spasms and she began to shake, she was silent during this period as waves and waves of orgasm hit her whole body. It took about five minutes for her whole body to calm so she could stand and she noticed my huge erection "your dick is huge she said in awe , I smiled and told her to bring it out and see how big it actually is, which she immediately did while kneeling down. When it was finally out ,I knew she was impressed cus she said ," hmmmmmm" and told me she likes big dicks and I said, "well you have one in your hands, what are you gonna do with it ?". She giggled and said, "watch and see". She then held my dick in her hands and began stroking and lubricating with saliva. Soon after, she took my cock deep into her throat and was making slurpy sounds and gagging on it while playing with my balls and I said to myself, this girl right here is a pornstar and smiled while holding her hair and using both hands to make a ponytail with it. She was really good at the *job*, so I was close to Cumming faster than usual and with fewer minutes, I came exploding streams and streams of thick hot cum deep into her throat. After I came, she continued sucking my dick, like she wanted to suck my soul out and my dick wasn't helping issues, as it was still rock hard, even harder with more veins, so I told her stop sucking and stand up, which she did. With my palm, I gently moved her back , giving her the signal to bend for a standing doggy style position and said "give me that pussy". With urgency, when did and was eager to get my dick inside her as she was moving her hips backward but, I decided not to give her what she wants just yet , and I began using my big dick to play with her clit, I'll use the dick to rub the outside of her pussy without moving it in, she was moaning gently and getting frustrated she had to look back at me with a needy eyes that shows how much she needs me in her, so I obliged to her inaudible request and slid the head of my cock inside her very wet pussy and she gasped. I wiggled the head of my cock inside of her, and brought it out, put the head in and brought it out again in a sec, I repeated this because I really wanted to tease her. She was getting sexual frustrated and she just had to speak , and she said "please put your dick in me and fuck me really hard" , at long last, that was the cue I have been waiting for, I slammed my dick into her at once, and instantly, he let out a loud squeam and she went into orgasm immediately I didn't stop thrusting into her pussy, I fucked her hard as she had requested with every thrust splashing her pussy juice in my body. After she had recovered from the orgasm, she started moving her hips back and meeting my thrust, and I pounded away. "This is the last scx I'm gonna be getting before I resume, and I'm gonna make it worthwhile" I thought as I continued giving the hostess a good fuck, and she assure me that she was enjoying every bit of it by giving a very sexy moan each time my balls hit her ass. Damn I didn't ask her name I said to myself laughing, imagine fucking a lady you just met and don't even know her name, well, I'll ask when we are done. She was getting closer to orgasm, as she was grinding me, making my dick go very deep and screaming harderrrr, fuck me baby, argggg, mmmmhhhmm, yessss, right there, fuck me, yes, fuck me baby, ahhhhh, yeahhh, yeahhh , with these, I rammed away giving in to all her requests, and I also felt myself getting close, and with all these words, I'll definitely cum faster, so I pounded hardest and deeper , and at that point, her pussy wall clenched my cock, and her body vibrating in my dick, her mouth open but she couldn't say a word as the orgasm swept through her entire body . At that point, I couldn't hold myself anymore, I released my load in her pussy while groaning and holding her slim waist. For five minutes, we were both still trying to catch our breath, and finally, she spoke to me and said "I'm not sure I will ever receive a fuck that good" , I didn't know what to say, so I just smiled and we began standing up and dressing, because after the orgasm, both of us were too exhausted to stand. After dressing up, she stood facing me, stared into my eyes and gave me a passionate kiss on the lips and I laughed and asked, "your boyfriend is gonna be mad for kissing me on the lips" she smiled and said, "who said I had a boyfriend" . Well I had to quickly leave the scene before things got emotionally out of hand cus I don't know what she was trying to insinuate. I was almost leaving , then I remembered again that I hadn't asked for her name , so I turned around and asked , she said Lisa, and further told me she lived in Massachusetts, wow nice, I go to school there, so we are going to see each other again after all. We exchanged contacts, and I went outside, and headed to my seat. When I sat down, my seat partner was fast asleep , probably from boredom. So I sat down, and proceeded to save Lisa's number on my phone and I guess she's doing the same in the toilet right now . After about three minutes, Lisa came out from the rest room, walked passed me with a pretty smile and a sexy wink and I noticed her hair was arranged, not well arranged tho, but not also scattered like someone who just received a good fuck, guess she arranges it will in the rest room. The rest of the journey was quite inventless as I played my football game, (the updated crappy version) which annoyed me to sleep after 10 minutes. Next I heard the pilot telling passengers to fasten the seatbelt as the plane was about to land. With my sleepy eyes, I alighted the plane and immediately saw my mom at the airport, looking all professionally dressed guessing she's coming from work, and we both headed to her SUV and drove home on the roads of New York.

Chapter 3 : IT WASN'T A BORING DAY AFTERALL.

Bored out of my mind, I mindlessly flip through the channels on the TV, hoping to find something good. I've already checked Netflix and was disappointed with the results, and this looks like it'll have the same outcome as well.

I knew coming back home would be boring. Especially after my second year of college, with the constant partying and hookups.

For the next three months, however, my life is gonna be nothing but taking night drives and hoping something interesting happens in this small town so I don't blow my brains out.

To be honest, the only interesting thing that has happened in the past two weeks that I've been home is getting to see my mom's friend, delia.

Well, she's actually fidelia, but with how close we are I've always just called her delia.

I'm not gonna mince words here, she's hot as hell. Ever since I was interested in women, she was the subject of my fantasies.

She's pretty tall, actually, but still shorter than me, something I've always teased her about. She's approximately 5'9", I'd estimate. She has great, round breasts, that I believe I've heard her call a C cup previously. Honestly, she could tell me any letter and I'd believe it. I'm a simple dude who enjoys boobs as well as adorned ass

Then there's her figure, she has more of a hourglass physique with an incredible ass. Like, 'it even fills out sweatpants perfectly' wonderful. She's also has a wonderful pair of hips that must be ideal for having babies.

And holding while fucking her. She's got shortish blonde hair, going down to her shoulders and a set of lovely blue eyes. She looks extremely amazing for her age, and the little of weight she has on her that she talks about all the time simply makes her hotter in my view. Cushion for the pushin, as they say.

Her spouse, Mr. Eric, I'm a bit less acquainted with. We don't hate one other at all, it's just that all our encounters are usually a bit short and uncomfortable. It's like we've never learned how to speak to one other.

delia, on the other hand? We got along nicely. It's like I could chat to her about anything. Girls, school issues, life, filthy jokes, you name it. This, of course, has led to our discussions growing rather... flirtatious over the previous two years. Not that I'm complaining, however. We both seem to enjoy it.

They've stayed the night a few times in the previous two weeks, so I had plenty opportunity to observe Delia's big ass in sweatpants or yoga pants going on by.

Sometimes I swear she would find reasons to walk past me many times, too.

I look outside, and the sun is already sinking.

Looks like it's even later than I anticipated, meaning another day has been squandered on boredom and awful TV series.

I groan, prepared to get up to either work out or play some video games upstairs, when I hear a banging on the glass.

I glance over, and it's delia, waving at me.

Happy to see her, and have something pleasant to do, I grin back and hurry outside to welcome her.

And what a terrific decision that was.

All she has on is an enormous shirt, possibly Mr. Eric's, and what I'm thinking to be a complete bikini suit below. I can just see the form of a skimpy, black bikini below the thin material of the shirt, but I can tell that she looks quite fine.

"Oh, wow." I blurt out, not even knowing it.

Delia only smiles at my answer.

"Well, I'm delighted someone loves it at least." she quips.

"Sorry, just a bit astonished. It's a little late to go swimming, don't you think?" I ask her.

She grins happily, bringing out a shopping bag full of booze from behind her.

"Well, I wasn't intending on utilizing y'pool. all's I was thinking about the hot tub." she adds.

The very concept of this makes my cock expand a bit in my trousers.

"Oh yeah?" I ask, unable to come up with a better retort.

"Yeah, I initially had your mom in mind, but she hasn't replied to my SMS or calls. So, I think you'll do." she teases.

I smirk, thanking the world for making me so blessed.

"I'll do it? delia, you know I'm a busy guy." I joke.

"Please." she replies, rolling her eyes. "Just go and get changed, it'll take a moment to set up the hot tub." she replies, turning away and making her way to the jacuzzi like she had been invited.

I have to admit, her confidence makes her much hotter to me.

Not wanting to waste another second, I walk upstairs fast, but on my approach to the stairs, I pass by my mom's room and discover something that completely cements the notion that I've been fortunate.

My Mom dropped out in bed, with a few empty bottles of alcohol on her nightstands.

Yup, she's been day-drinking.

And she's out cold.

Which implies no one will disturb us while we're conversing.

I make my way to my room even quicker, changing into one of my more, as I call it, 'sluttier' pair of swim trunks. The legs aren't as long, and it's tighter than my others, providing a decent indication of what I'm dealing with.

I look myself out in the mirror as though I'm suddenly going to be less cut than normal.

Fortunately, I've built up an excellent habit of working out and exercising regularly, meaning that I have a nicely formed and toned figure, guaranteed to garner some praises out of delia.

Then, there's the fact that I have a very visible bulge. I'm approximately four inches soft, getting to a max of seven when I'm hard. I'm really delighted with it, and it's never garnered anything but praises from the ladies I've been with.

So to sum it up, I'm dressing up as much as I can in swim trunks for my mom's buddy.

Luckily, Delia can keep a secret.

I slip downstairs, being careful to not make any extra sounds and risk waking up my mom, gently locking the door to the backyard behind me.

I attempt to slowly up the path to the jacuzzi, as hard as it is to resist the impulse to sprint so I can see Delia in her bikini as soon as possible. I manage to withstand these temptations, strolling like a regular human being up to the hot tub.

Unfortunately, Delia was already sitting in it, evidently enjoying herself in the warm, calming water.

That is, until she saw me go out.

Her eyes widen, and her cheeks grow even redder.

"Oh, my!" she exclaims. "When the heck did you become so... cut?! You could shred flesh on those abs!" she exclaims, laughing from the astonishment.

Yep, just the response I intended.

I keep my cool, smirking confidently.

"Well, I didn't want you to be the only one to be revealing that much flesh." I say, stepping into the hot tub. "Although, I believe you've got me beat." I taunt, grabbing for a drink.

She grins at this.

"Wow, simply going behave like that and take a drink right in front of me? I should inform your mum!" she quips. "But I won't." she adds, taking a drink of her beer.

"Hey - I could always take it off if you think it's too much." I flirt.

She starts to fan herself humorously.

"Please, it's already hot enough in this tub. Anymore and I fear I'd start boiling." she laughs.

Despite seeming cool and collected, I'm freaking out on the inside. The lady I've been pining on for years is seated across from me in a tiny bikini, flirting with me. Fuck, this is nearly too much.

"So," she says, drinking her drink. "How about you tell your closest buddy how college is going. Any nice females you may bring home to your mom?" she says. "Because you better not. That'd hurt my heart watching my fave boyfriend being taken up like that." she taunts.

I roll my eyes humorously.

"Well, it's largely just been a bunch of hookups, actually. Not looking for anything too serious with any females at school just now. I've been asked to a fairly decent number of parties too, so that's fantastic." I say, taking a gulp of my beer. "And I made the Dean's List." I boast.

Delia's eyes widened at this, a look of pride on her face.

"Oh, look at you! Smart and popular, huh? No surprise you've been having an easy time with the females there!" she chuckles.

"Please, you're going make me blush." I joke.

Delia has always been there to pump me up, and it's really boosted my confidence growing up. Of course, lately it's become more like flirting.

Obviously I have no issues with this, however.

"Still a bashful little child, huh?" she teases, scooting closer to me in the hot tub. "And here I'd assumed you'd become accustomed to an old woman's flattery after being around all those floozies at school." she laughs.

"'Floozies'?" I answer, chuckling. "You're not doing yourself any favours." I tease. "Besides, you had all those females at college beaten. I'd have a really hard time concentrating in class if they all looked nearly as wonderful as you." I flirt, feeling more ballsy as she moves closer to me.

She grins, her cheeks growing slightly crimson.

"Is that right? Well, it's a good thing they don't" she teases, scooting right up close to me. "I'd hate to have you act up and destroy those fine scores." she continues, her voice more enticing now.

Fuck, I'm ready to act up now.

"Honestly, I believe my grades could suffer a few blows if it meant I'd get to have you to gaze at." I flirt.

She chuckles at this.

"And what about me is so distracting?" she replies, turning to face me, her breasts pressing up on my arm now.

"Shit, all of you. Did you not get a good look in the mirror when putting that bikini on?" I say, my cock growing in my trunks.

She chuckles once more, staring at me with comfortable, if not eager, eyes.

"I mean, I've always thought you were attractive as hell. You've got such a gorgeous face, particularly those adorable blue eyes of yours. Could look at them for hours." I told her.

"Such a charmer." she grins.

"And you know I gotta say something about that body of yours." I laugh.

"Of course, you could scarcely take your eyes off of me all night." she quips.

"God, you have such a lovely figure. Like, the right sort of thick." I say.

"Two C's?" she laughs.

"Two C's. For sure." I react with a chuckle myself. "I mean, you've got an ass that looks fantastic even in sweatpants. Can't even begin to tell you how pleased I'd be when you'd come over in leggings. Or anything that showed off your legs." I told her.

"Glad you were paying attention. My spouse doesn't seem to recognize my... endowments." she chuckles, appearing a bit sorry about her marriage.

Well, screw him. He's an idiot.

"Shit, you'll always be recognized by me. You're too darn attractive to not notice." I told her.

"Aren't you the sweetest... Are you sure there's nothing more you want tell me?" she implies, squeezing her breasts against my arms more.

I giggle at this.

"Who could forget how wonderful your boobs look? I've thought about them being mashed up against me so many stinking times." I tell her, my cock now totally erect.

"And are they as nice as you imagined?" she says.

"It's much greater than I ever expected." I responded.

She grins, obviously not wanting to stop at any time soon.

We both stare up at the sky, since the sun has already long ago set. The hot tub is nice and the bubbles are as peaceful as you'd assume they are. It certainly helps when you have a lovely lady pushing her chest against your arm.

Delia is laying her head on me, no longer facing me and but using my arm as something to grab onto as if she'd drift away. As for my hand, it's now resting on her inner thigh, softly squeezing it.

Fuck, even touching her thigh feels like a dream.

"There's really a lot more I've thought about with you, too." I shatter the stillness.

"Oh yeah? And what's that?" she wonders, still peering up.

"I'll give you one, but then you gotta start talking to yourself." I tease.

"Fine, jerk!" she jokes.

"To be honest, I've always thought your height was attractive. Like, towering ladies are simply attractive as heck." I told her.

"Well, I wasn't exactly anticipating that response." she laughs. "Must be because you still tower over me nonetheless." she flirts.

She huffs, and smirks a little.

"You know, I think my husband kind of hates that we're the same height." she confesses.

"Oh yeah? Why do you say that?" I inquire.

"Well, for starters, he doesn't let me wear heels. Not even at our wedding!" she exclaims.

"Damn, really?" I inquire, oblivious of how insecure he actually was.

"Yes! I mean, I had to wear flats! Flats!" she moans.

"That's a shame. I imagine you'd look really fucking stunning with some heels. Especially a wedding dress." I told her.

"You bet your ass I would. And that outfit looked wonderful on me!" she adds, giggling.

"Maybe you should show me some time." I flirt.

She's taken a little off guard by this, but laughs it off.

"Easy there, jack. Keep talking so beautifully and I just may." she teases.

I chuckle, trying to ignore the raging erection that's threatening to tear through my trunks.

"Now, I guess I've talked enough for now. How about you start opening up?" I ask, grinning at her.

She giggles.

"Alright, playboy. Just go and force some poor old woman to tell you what you already know." she taunts. "Well, one thing I've always enjoyed was that voice of yours - so deep and... seductive." she teases, attempting to replicate my voice with the last word.

"Oh yeah? Well, it must be why you let me speak so much." I joke.

"Please, you could read a phone book and I'd listen to every word." she says.

"Come on over more, then. I could read anything you want." I joke.

"Don't tempt me with a good time!" she jokes. "Now, what else was there... God, this body!" she exclaims, putting a hand on my chest. "You've always looked good, but you seriously look like you could throw me around!" she says, feeling my abs now,

She runs her hand all along my torso, feeling how toned and fit I am.

"Fuck, those shoulders and arms of yours are too gorgeous to not praise. It fucking kills me when you pull your sleeves up and I see those huge veins on your arms!" she adds, grabbing my forearm.

"Maybe I should do it more frequently." I flirt.

"I speak for all the ladies in the community when I say this: Please!" she shouts.

I giggle at this, feeling my ego become greater with each praise.

"And finally-" she starts, shifting herself to straddle me, looking at me with our faces mere inches apart. "- This gorgeous face of yours." she says, grabbing my cheeks and squishing them with one hand.

I'm sure she can feel my cock grinding against her, as she's pressing down against my lap.

"Now, how about you tell me some more, jacky?" she whispers, pressing down more against my cock to emphasise the 'big boy'.

I giggle at this, trying to play it cool.

Fuck, I want her so bad.

"I've always thought about you taking your top off and letting me see and feel your tits." I bluntly tell her, feeling like there's no reason to not be forward.

"You disgusting guy!" she fakes. "Thinking about your mom's friend that way?!" she says, leaning back some, her hands reaching behind her back. "You were thinking about a woman old enough to be your mother and take her top off?" she says, fiddling behind her back. "Just like this?" she says in a sweeter tone, her top falling into the water, exposing her bare tits.

My eyes darted down to them, and they're just as great as I imagined.

They're the perfect size. She has pink, plump nipples and delicate, white skin. Her breasts are enormous, and honestly lovely looking. I've seen a lot of tits, particularly since I've been away at college, and none of them could compare to the pair in front of me.

It helps that they belong to an older, sexier lady.

"Holy fuck..." I gasp, unable to take my eyes off of them.

She giggles, enjoying my response.

"Don't be bashful, jack. How about you touch them some?" she purrs, sliding her fingers through my hair.

I don't need to be told twice. My hands run up along her hips and along her sides, tracing her until they get to her soft, round breasts. I squeeze them gently at first, still unable to believe this is all real.

She moans slightly, giggling afterwards.

"Mmmm... I love your touch..." she tells me.

With her sitting on top of me, her fingers running through my hair, and being able to play with her soft, wonderful tits, I feel like I'm king of the universe.

I continue to play with them a bit more, my fingers now wandering to her nipples and squeezing them little, feeling them tighten.

"That's it..." she groans.

"Does... does Mr. Eric know about any of this?" I ask, as if any response would stop me.

"Please, don't worry about him, baby. Our bedroom has been dead for quite a while." she says. "And with your mother being out of commission, I think it's just you and me tonight. Just what I wanted." she purrs.

"Oh yeah?" I ask, still playing with her nipples.

She groans in form of a yes.

"You think I didn't know she'll pass out? Your mom wouldn't stop talking about her plans for today, so I figured she'd be passed out after a few bottles of wine by this time." she adds.

Now that she says it, it seemed a touch too handy.

"You didn't think I'd bring this scant little thing when I knew they'd both be awake, would you?" she asks, continuing to press against my cock with her butt. "No, baby.

This was all for you." she whispers in my ear, kissing it.

"For me?" I dumbly ask, too stimulated to think of a better response.

"That's correct. You have no idea how many times I'd go home after flirting with you when I visited, wet and frustrated." she tells me. "And my husband would either be passed out or at work, allowing me to fuck myself crazy with a vibrator, thinking about you the whole time." she sighs in my ear.

"Fuck, delia..." I groan.

"It was so hard not to think these things about you. I mean, you became so large and hot... God, the day I watched you climb out of the water and those trunks clung to you, giving everyone a perfect glimpse of your bulge, fuck it drove me insane!" she says. "And then there was that time I spotted that box of jumbo condoms, stashed beneath your pillow. Enough was peeping through that I could figure out what it was." she murmurs. "And it took everything in me to not jump your bones right then and there." she tells me.

"I was hoping you'd see it. I concealed it that way so you could see it." I confess, smirking.

"You little sneak!" she grins. "But tonight-" she continues, putting her face closer to mine. "No condoms. No interruptions." she says. "Just you and me." she adds, kissing me.

I promptly reciprocate. The kiss is hungry and passionate, obvious that we've both been wanting this for a while. We groan into our lips as our tongues contact and begin to dance.

Her fingers are sliding through my hair again, as she's attempting to shove my face into hers as much as possible.

My hands instead slide down to her shapely ass, gripping it and keeping her close to me as we kiss.

Hearing her speak like that drove me nuts. Mr. Eric is an idiot for disregarding her like way. Fortunately, I'll take excellent care of her. After kissing for what feels like hours, we break it off, a string of saliva connecting our mouths.

"Now fuck me silly, college boy. Make me your woman under the stars." she says.

To say the least, that got a reaction out of me.

I lift her up out of the water, sitting her on the edge of the hot tub so that her legs still stay in.

"Looks like you really can throw me around." she says, biting her lower lip.

I push her back some, reaching for the skimpy bikini bottom and pushing it to the side. I bring my mouth close to the already wet entrance, and begin to gently tongue at it.

"And you eat pussy without being told? God, I am gonna have some fun with you, jackie." she giggles, with slightly surprised moans escaping at the end. "Show me what you learned from those sluts at school." she says, putting one hand on the back of my head.

With pleasure, I think to myself.

I reach up and slide two fingers inside of her, surprised at how wet she already is. I slowly slide them in and out, enjoying how delia feels wrapped around my fingers.

"Mmmmm, I can't even tell you how long I've been wet. I think I first started to feel it when you walked out in those trunks..." she moans, shifting to get comfortable I begin to kiss back up her thigh to the entrance of her cunt, feeling her jump slightly each time.

She giggles, and moves around some more at this.

"Fuck, I don't think I've ever been so sensitive to something like a kiss on the thigh..." she says, her breath shaky.

Without another word, I begin to gently tease her clit with the tip of my tongue, the taste sweet and intoxicating.

"Mmm! And you actually know where it's at?" she giggles. "Baby, you're already doing better than my husband!"

Damn, really? They've been married that long and he couldn't find something as easy to find as the clit? No wonder she's cheating.

Guess I have him to thank for tonight, though.

I begin to work my fingers inside of her, rubbing my fingertips against her g-spot.

She coos in pleasure, her hand travelling to the back of my head.

She's wrapped tight around my fingers, and she's already practically dripping wet.

Being able to eat my hot mom's friend out, combined with the warm and relaxing water from the hot tub covering me, this night feels otherworldly. Her gentle moans and noises of pleasure are too great to even describe.

What makes it even better is knowing that I'm the reason she's making these noises.

I begin to finger her faster, combined with circling her clit with my tongue at a rhythmic, steady pace. These two actions combined earns even louder moans from her.

"Thank god your mom is knocked out... I'd hate to have to try and keep quiet." she says in between her moans of pleasure.

I reach up with my free hand and begin to pinch and stimulate one of her nipples, feeling it get even harder in between my fingers.

Delia then sits up, and I shift myself and my fingers so as not to pause my rhythm.

She grabs my hand, pulling it to her mouth, where she begins to suck on my fingers. I can feel her moans vibrate through her closed mouth onto my fingers, and they get louder the harder I work my fingers.

She stares down at me, her blue eyes struggling to keep fully open the longer I tongue her clit. I know she's just sucking my fingers, but I can't help but think this is the sexiest thing ever.

Her warm tongue licks and wraps around my finger, all the while she sucks in. Fuck, I'd love for it to be my cock instead. I wonder how much of it she could handle?

My thought process is broken when she moans loudly, freeing my finger from her mouth.

"Fuck~!" she moans, the hand on the back of my head gripping my hair tighter.

I ignore what little pain is caused by her grip, and keep my pace going, knowing what'll be coming soon.

"Please don't stop, baby!" she begs. "Please!" her voice getting whinier and more strained.

I can start to feel her tighten around my fingers, and she's getting more fidgety.

"Make me cum jackiiee, you little stud!" she moans, biting her lip. "Fuck, you're gonna make me cum so hard!" she says.

I try to make sure I'm focusing on using both my tongue and fingers equally, making sure she's getting equal amounts of pleasure in both areas.

And it seems to be working, as her pussy is now repeatedly gripping and loosening around my fingers as she squirms more.

"Oh fuck! Oh fuck, baby!" she moans, her voice louder this time.

The pulsating gets more rapid, and her moans become more incomprehensible and wild, with heavy breathing becoming more and more prevalent.

Finally, the tightening stops, and her moans disappear, replaced now with her panting. Delia then lays back on the ground, her chest rising and lowering again and again.

I slide my fingers out of her, with the two of them glistening with her juices. I lift my head up and out from in between her legs, and look at my handiwork.

There in front of me lies a sexy, mature woman. Who also happens to be married and also my mom's friend. Her skimpy bikini top is currently floating in the hot tub, with her bare, perfectly shaped tits rising with each breath. The stringy bikini bottom is pushed to the side, with her trimmed and tight cunt exposed to my eyes only.

Her breathing calms down, and she begins to speak.

"You made me cum..." she pants. "So. Fucking. Fast." she says in disbelief. "What the hell are they teaching you at college?!" she laughs.

"Seems like how to treat a woman." I flirt, climbing out and kissing her on her nipple, sucking and teasing it with my tongue.

She giggles, putting her hands on the back of my head and pushing me in deeper. Light moans came from her in response to my tongue.

"Obviously. You must be making a LOT of women happy there, huh?" she asks, still playing with my hair.

I continue to suck and tease her tits, enjoying the feeling of having them in my mouth. Her dainty fingers continue to be stroking my hair as I do so.

"Alright, college boy. Take those trunks off and sit down. It's time I repay you for your... services." she jokes.

"With pleasure, ma'am." I retorted.

I stand up, dropping my trunks with ease.

My fully erect cock springs out, fortunately with no shrinkage due to the hot tub being, well, hot.

Once Delia sets her eyes on it, they widen from shock.

"No fucking way." she says in disbelief. "T-that's REAL?!" she says, starting to laugh.

"Last time I checked." I joke. "Sexy women in bikinis tend to make it like this."

She laughs at this.

"Then I'll just have to take responsibility for it, huh?" she says. "After all, something this big, you might get dizzy from all that blood rushing to it." she purrs. "So sit down on the edge of the tub and let me take care of it." she tells me, getting in the warm water once again.

I sit down, feeling the excitement build up inside of me. Eating her out is one thing, but getting a blowjob from her? Unreal.

She positions herself in between my legs, and gently wraps her dainty fingers around the shaft of my cock.

"It's so... big! Like, some guys are long and some guys are thick, but you're both!" she exclaims.

"Biggest yet?" I tease.

"Honey, this thing is a monster!" she responds. "Luckily, I don't get scared so easily." she says, licking up my shaft.

I shudder from the feeling of her warm tongue sliding up the length of my cock.

"Guessing it's a lot bigger than your husband, huh?" I taunt.

She looks up at me and smirks.

"I think we both know the answer to that one, baby." she tells me.

"C'mon, I wanna hear you say it." I tell her, putting one hand on the back of head.

She giggles a little at this.

"You're a cocky little shit, aren't you?" she teases. "But yes, you are MUCH bigger than him. Both in length and width." she says.

"And I can't wait to feel how it fits inside of me..." she moans, licking my length again.

Stopping the conversation, delia takes me into her mouth, her lips gently wrapping around the head of my cock first before she tries to fit as much inside as possible.

She can only get a little over half of it in her mouth, not that I'm complaining. Even an inch of it inside of her mouth would beat the girls at college that could deep throat it.

She bobs her head up and down, being careful to not go too deep and gag.

"Fuck, delia..." I moan, watching her work her mouth along my cock. "It feels so good..." I told her.

She giggles as a reply, and I can feel the vibrations along my cock as she does so.

Then, she begins to use her tongue while sucking, heightening the sensation.

"Oh!" I let out in surprise.

Delia is too busy focusing on not gagging to make a comment, and continues to use her tongue to pleasure me.

It feels even better than I imagined. Whenever I fantasised about this, it was always her coming into my room one night and making a move, not inviting me out to the hot tub where we'd flirt and slowly start to touch each other more and more.

I prefer it this way, though. It's much hotter than my initial fantasies, but it also helps that this one is coming true.

"Sorry it's not as deep as you're probably used to." she says, seeming a bit disappointed in herself. "I don't exactly have much practice with one this big." she says with a wink, kissing the head of my cock.

I shiver from the feeling, and chuckle.

"Please, the fact that you're the one doing it makes this the best one I've ever had." I told her.

"Is that right?" she asks. "Even better than all those girls you partied with?" she teases, running her tongue in circles along the top of my head.

"They can't even begin to compare to you." I say, moaning.

"Good answer." she says, taking my cock deeper in her mouth once again.

Not a single lie was told, either. I'm sorry, but girls my age just can't compete with delia. A hot, sexually frustrated housewife who wants MY cock? Yeah, sorry.

I lean my head back, looking up at the sky while Delia pleasures me with her mouth. Every now and then I'd look down, her bright blue eyes looking up at me, and a slight smile would form at the corners of her mouth.

At least, I think it's a smile. It's kind of hard to tell when she's got her lips wrapped around a thick rod.

She continues bobbing her head up and down, getting faster and faster every second. I can hear the sounds of her gagging and moaning on my cock, and it's taking everything in me to not cum at this very moment.

"Oh- shit!" I moan.

Delia takes her hand and wraps it around my shaft, acting as a sort of guard to stop her from going too far and gagging.

Her tongue continues to lick and wrap around my cock as she sucks, creating an indescribable feeling of pleasure.

I start to shake a little bit from the pleasure, but delia suddenly stops, a string of saliva connecting her lips to the tip of my cock.

"Sorry, college boy. I didn't wanna stop either, but I'm not gonna let you cum and have it stop with just oral." she says, climbing out of the water and on top of me.

She shoves her bikini bottoms to the side once again, and reaches down and grabs my cock.

"You don't get to cum unless it's inside of me and I'm screaming, no, begging for you to understand?" she says.

Fuck, she's so sexy when she acts like this.

"Yes, ma'am." I answer, excited to slide inside of her.

"Good boy." she replies, kissing me quickly on the lips before sliding the tip of my cock into her entrance.

It's tight, warm, and wet. It's everything I imagined and more. Slowly, she slides down along my shaft, reaching the base and resting for a bit.

"Oh- I feel full." she says, laughing slightly. "Fuck, you're really filling me up in there, huh?" she softly moans.

"Need some time to get used to it?" I tease.

"Oh yeah. Something this big I gotta get used to..." she says, making a circle with her hips. "God, you're gonna stretch me out so bad." she states.

"Got a problem with that?" I ask.

"Fuck no. You can use that big cock to do whatever you want to this tight little hole, got it?" she tells me.

"I plan to." I answer, enjoying the feeling of her sex tightly wrapped around my cock.

"Look at you. So smart, knowing just what to say." she teases. "I'll have to think of some way to reward you." she says, beginning to slowly lift her hips up and down.

"As if this isn't one?" I flatter.

"True, but I've got a couple things in mind." she tells me. "It's a surprise, though." she whispers, leaning in and giving me a quick kiss.

She sits up straight, her hands on my chest to act as support while she slowly adjusts to the new length and girth inside of her.

"Good thing I have such a sturdy and hard place to keep my hands." she flirts, not taking her eyes off of me while she speaks.

I watch as her cunt slowly lifts up, almost rising off of my cock, before slowly sliding back down, delia moaning all the while.

"God, baby..." she purrs.

She begins to ride slightly faster, getting used to the thick rod inside of her.

"That's it..." I moan, reaching up and pinching her nipples.

This earns a moan of pleasure in response.

The sound of her body slapping down onto mine gets louder and louder the more ready she gets. Her cunt has managed to get even wetter, with my cock now lubed up to make sure she has an easy time sliding up and down my long dick.

"You like that dick, baby?" I ask.

"Fuck, yes!" she moans, her riding getting faster.

"Good, because I love your pussy..." I moan as she keeps riding.

She closes her eyes from the pleasure, nodding as she continues to bounce up and down, her pace now much faster than it was originally.

Her tits bounce up and down as she does so, and I'm sure her perfect ass is as well, if only I could see it from behind in this position.

She alternates between looking at me and keeping her eyes clenched shut, unable to stick to one.

"God, I never knew how good a big dick could feel!" she exclaims, seemingly still shocked. "I might have jumped your bones a long time ago if I knew it'd be this good." she says.

"Younger me would have loved that." I answer, moaning myself.

"I bet, bagging some hot housewife? Now look at you, watching that same woman riding your big, fat cock." she laughs, her body slapping down onto mine each time she slides down.

"All while in the backyard of my house while my mom is sleeping." I tease.

I feel her tighten around my cock once I say that, and I start to realise she likes how dangerous this is.

"Oh, you like that, don't you?" I tease.

She giggles, not slowing down.

"You like fucking your friend's son in her own backyard? Using her hot tub so you could get fucked while she sleeps?" I taunt.

Her cunt tightens even more.

"Yes..." she coyly admits, now moaning louder.

"What a naughty friend you are." I say, teasing her nipples once again, her tits bouncing in my hands. "And a bad, bad wife." I told her.

She moans louder from this, and I can feel her tightening once again.

"You love being called out for this, huh? Cheating on your husband for some thick, young dick?" I ask, her pace starting to speed up.

"Fuck, baby..." she moans. "I'm a bad girl..." she says, smiling.

"That's right, you're a bad little housewife that needs to get fucked." I say.

"Good thing I have my - oh fuck..." she moans, interrupting herself. "At least I have a good college boy to fuck some sense into me..." she says.

"I'll make you loyal to my cock." I say, my voice deep and dominant.

"I think you already have, baby..." she says, her voice breathy and shaky.

Her hands on my chest, she begins to practically slam herself down on my cock, and I feel her warm, wet hole tighten wildly each time.

"Fuck..." she moans, her voice getting whinier at the end.

I pinch her nipples harder and I watch her amazing body jiggle every time she slams down. Her nipples are hard in between my fingers now, and Delia looks like she can barely keep focus because of the pleasure contorting her face.

The sound of her slapping down onto my cock has gotten louder, and surely the neighbours will hear it if they step outside. Fortunately, our moans and bodies hitting each other passionately isn't enough to wake my mom out of her drunken slumber.

"Fuck, delia. You look so good bouncing on that dick..." I tell her, my voice breaking from the moaning.

"Do I, baby? Maybe I should make a habit of doing this, then." she giggles, biting her lip and rotating her hips on me.

"I'll always be down to let you." I respond, pushing my hips up as she slides back down.

"Maybe I'll just sneak in your room late at night wearing a little skirt so you can hitch it up easier..." she moans.

"Fuck, there's a lot of things I'd like to see you in..." I chuckle.

"Oh yeah?" she moans. "And what's that, college boy?" she asks, enjoying hearing how desired she is by me.

"Fuck, I've thought of maid costumes, teacher costumes, playboy bunny costumes... you name it, really." I told her.

"You naughty boy... I love it." she says, moaning. "Maybe I'll surprise you one day." she giggles.

I feel my balls tighten from the thought of that.

"Fuck, I'd leave you sore and walking funny if you did." I laugh.

"As if that's not what you're gonna do to me tonight?" she giggles, bouncing up and down quickly.

She slides up and down on my shaft for a while longer, before her pace gets sloppier and she starts to slow down.

"Baby, I'm sorry... This feels fucking amazing, but it's really starting to tire me out..." she moans, out of breath.

"Don't worry, I'll take it from here." I tell her, lifting up.

She slides up off of my cock, it now glistening from her wetness.

"Get on your hands and knees." I order, giving her a sharp smack on the ass.

She exclaims in excitement, before giggling like a schoolgirl.

"Mmmm, yes sir." she says, getting into position.

She laid a towel out on the ground before doing so, making it more comfortable than just the bare concrete ground around the tub.

I get situated behind her, grabbing her ass with both hands and spreading it more.

"Take a good look, baby. That ass belongs to you, now.

"I'm going watch this thing bounce as I fuck you." I tell her, spanking her.

I carefully push my cock inside of her, seeing her tight lips take me in and grasp me all the time.

She gives out a low sigh of satisfaction as I enter inside of her, and she softly starts to sway her hips to make me move.

I grasp her by her soft hips and gently begin to pump it in and out of her.

"Fuck, you fill me up so nice... It's like that cock was meant for me..." she chuckles.

"And your pussy feels so nice wrapped around me." I say, pounding somewhat faster now.

Each time I push in fully, I see a ripple being transmitted through her exquisitely sculpted ass.

"Everything you imagined?" she asks, staring back at me with a smug smile.

"Yeah, your ass is great." I tell her, grasping it with one hand.

"You know precisely how to speak to a woman." she says, smiling.

I laugh, and continue to fuck harder, eliciting even more murmurs of approbation from her. At least I can always tell whether she loves it or not based on how noisy she is.

Her ass is now jiggling much more as I'm going quicker and harder, and it's impossible to keep my eyes off of it. I give her a swift smack on the ass, shocking her.

A faint, crimson hand print appears on her ass from it.

I can do better.

I smack again, harder.

"Oh, baby!" she groans.

The hand print is redder now.

And I slap her again. And again. And again.

Each time my palm smashes against her naked ass, I feel her clench around my cock. The tiny harlot.

"Oh- fuck!" she lets out.

The hand print is now red and visible.

"Just designating it as mine." I joke, fucking her quicker.

"Mmmmm, can't wait for you to brand me on the inside..." she groans.

Damn, she's filthy. How did I become so lucky?

Delia's cries of delight bring me back to reality.

"That's it, sweetie... Please don't stop." she begs, gritting her teeth from the pleasure. "Fuck this little whore housewife... make her yours..." she coos.

I smirk. I'm really making her speak like this, aren't I?

"Yeah, you're a little slut of a housewife, you know that?" I say, spanking her.

She tightens fast from this.

"Just a tiny whore who wants some young, strong dick." I tell her, grabbing a clump of hair. "Cheating on her spouse with some college man..." I pull her hair back, receiving another sigh of delight from her.

"Yesssss!" she exclaims.

"How does it feel to be the slut of someone half your age?" I ask, smacking her ass. "I asked you a question, whore." I spank her ass again, another handprint appearing on her other cheek now.

"It- oh fuck!" she gasps, unable to speak properly from how rapidly I'm fucking her now. "It feels so fucking nice... you make me feel like a lady again..." she says.

"Good girl. You're my lady now, got it? This pussy belongs to me." I told her.

She tries nodding her head in return, only able to groan madly now.

"Use that pussy whatever you want." she eventually gets out. "It's yours, darling!" she shouts. I keep hammering my cock in and out of her, her tight cunt eagerly swallowing every inch. Her ass is now bouncing fast, crimson with two obvious handprints on each of her cheeks. Looks like I've done a good enough job of designating her ass as mine.

I give her another hard spank.

Doesn't mean I have to quit, however.

With one hand holding her hair back and the other gripping her hips, I keep slamming in and out from behind. She's doing her best to not scream, yet trying to not go full out and risk waking my mom.

"Fuck, baby..." she groans.

I can feel her clenching on my cock.

I know what's coming next.

Problem is, I'm coming close too.

"I know sweetie... I'm near, too." I told her.

"Cum with me... please, cum with me!" she pleads.

I smile.

Looks like I've received authorization now.

"Yeah? You want cum with me?" I taunt, hitting her on the ass.

"Y-yes!" she begs.

"You going cum hard for me when I start filling you up?" I ask.

I felt her stiffen more more along my big cock from this.

"Please! Yes!" she groans.

"Good fucking chick..." I groan, my hips smashing into her harder.

I continue to fuck her, her hot cunt constricting around my cock even more than it had on my fingers before.

She's coming closer, and so am I.

I can feel my balls tightening, and the only thing going through my thoughts is filling her up and formally branding her as my lady.

Animalistic, I know.

"Fuck! Fuck fuck fuck FUCK!" she shouts.

I keep ramming my cock in and out of her, still gripping a handful of her hair.

"Cum with me, darling! Please, fucking shoot it inside of me!" she pleads.

That's cnough to send me over the brink.

Her cunt starts to hold and release my cock swiftly, and her moans and utterances have grown more incoherent. As she cums on my cock, I begin to fire my full inside of her.

"Fuck, delia!" I let go, spraying rope after rope of my hot cum inside of her.

Her moans are now screams of ecstasy now, and her body is trembling from all of it.

I keep pounding my cock in and out, continuously spewing out inside of her.

Finally, after what seems like hours of cumming together, her cunt relaxes further and I finally fire my last shot of cum inside of her.

Our breathing is harsh and quick, and we've both worked up a sweat throughout our brief romance.

"Oh..." she sighs.

I carefully slipped my cock out of her, now gleaming from our fluids.

I sit back on the towel, my cock beginning to soften.

Delia is still on her hands and knees, her ass up and face down. I see my seed start to stream out of her.

"Fuck, delia..." I murmur, reaching out and softly stroking her ass with one hand.

After a few more seconds of relaxation, Delia sits back up and turns to face me, leaning back and keeping herself up with her hands.

We gaze at one other closely for a time, until she slides back onto me and we kiss passionately.

Our sweaty, sticky bodies are jammed up against one other. The two of us are still filthy and sweaty after the intercourse, but neither of us care.

Our tongues dance once more in our lips, and we groan into one other's mouths, not wanting to break the kiss.

I run a hand through her hair, smoothing out some of the knots that occurred from when I effectively used her earlier.

Finally, she pulls away, a rope of saliva joining our tongues.

We look each other in our eyes again, before we start to giggle gently.

"You were great." I told her.

She giggles gently.

"I'd say you were the impressive one. You and that third leg of yours." she quips, grasping my sensitive cock.

"You were the one who treated it so lovingly." I respond with a smirk.

She chuckles, sitting alongside me and leans against me.

We both glance up into the night sky, heat still radiating off of us.

"You're such a nasty talker, you know that?" she asks. "I mean, whore this, slut that." she chuckles.

"And you appeared to enjoy it a lot." I answer with a smirk.

"Oh, I liked it. Felt like you were using me." she tells me. "It was freaking hot." she chuckles.

"You know what was hot? How you appeared on top. And from behind. And on your knees." I continue, giggling.

"I felt fairly attractive when I held a large dick in my hands. Or my mouth. Or within me." she copies.

I giggle, kissing her again.

After shattering it, she speaks out.

"We should probably get cleaned up." she adds. "And I should probably get home." she moans.

"Not gonna spend the night with me? My bed is large enough." I say.

"Don't tempt me, sweetie." she kisses me on the cheek, standing up. "Maybe I'll have to concoct an excuse to slip away for the night while your mom is out town, however. She's a workaholic, so that would be simple" she replies with a smile.

I stand up as well, and she gathers our clothing.

"Now, if I know your mom well enough, she's probably still passed out. So how about we take a good shower and clean up?" she says.

I nod, wanting to see her soaped up and wet.

"Good guy. After that, I'll return home and probably sleep all day tomorrow to... recuperate." she says, her walking is wobbly.

I move behind her, taking a hold of her ass.

"Don't worry, I got you." I told her.

"What a gentleman!" she quips.

We sneak inside the home, still naked, and tiptoe upstairs to my bathroom.

Sure enough, my mum is still in her room, passed up and snoring.

Once we go to the restroom, we shut and lock the door, just in case.

Delia throws the now cum-stained towel in the hamper, and spreads our clothing out on the counter.

I turn the shower on, and we both hop in once it becomes warm.

Admittedly, much of the shower was simply us soaping one other up and groping each other. Fortunately, this still helped us get cleaned up.

Since I was too fatigued to get it back up, and Delia was too worn out to want to go for a second round, nothing very remarkable occurred in that shower.

Except seeing her all soaped up and shining. Gotta admit, toying with a big ass and gorgeous tits is a lot more enjoyable when there's suds involved.

We idly talked away the whole time as well, then we got off and dried off.

Once clothed, we slipped back downstairs and outside while I took her to her vehicle.

She placed her items in the passenger seat, and she remained to chat to me some longer.

"So it wasn't a one time occurrence, right?" I ask.

She laughs.

"After what you done to me? Baby, there's no lady in the world that could maintain it as a one time thing." she tells me.

"And um... what about my ending inside of you?" I ask, only now understanding how perilous that may be.

She chuckles at this, too.

"Please, baby. I wouldn't let you cum inside if I couldn't manage it. Trust me, I don't want to be raising another baby at my age." she laughs.

I feel great now, even more so since I get to keep cumming inside of her.

She stretches, sighing as I hear her back pop.

"Well, I should probably head home now. Wouldn't want my hubby to start wondering why I remained so late." she says.

Disappointing, but I understand.

She puts her arms around me, kissing me.

I kiss back, getting another feel of her ass while doing so.

She laughs, smacking my chest humorously.

"Little perv!" she says.

"You like it." I smile.

She rolls her eyes and smirks.

"Yeah. I think." she cynically remarks.

She unlocks the door to her vehicle and jumps inside, rolling down her window after turning it on.

"I've got your number so... how about we plan out some additional meetings?" she says.

Fuck. Yes.

"Yeah, contact me when you get home, yeah?" I told her.

She nods.

"I had a lot of fun tonight. Like... a lot of fun." she tells me.

I grin at her.

"And I had a lot of fun too. I want do this again. Soon." I said to her,

"Don't worry, I'm not gonna have you wait that long." she replies with a smile. "But now, I really should go home." she sighs.

"Good night then, delia." I told her.

"Good night, college guy. Try to not milk your sheets thinking about me tonight." she chuckles.

I laugh as she backs out of the driveway, observing her the whole time.

As I watch her drive out of view, I start to grasp how fatigued I was.

I go back inside and to bed, lying down.

After around 10 minutes, Delia contacts me.

We start to banter back and forth over text stupidly till I fall asleep.

But tomorrow, that's when we schedule a fresh meeting.

But that's another tale for another time.

Chapter 4: TWICE THE CHARM

I have been told I'm a spoiled brat, well, what do you expect from an incredibly handsome young man like myself who always gets what he wants. My dad and mom aren't broke, they have a few millions in their accounts and I usually get what I want , if money can buy it . I'm not really an outside person, but when I'm around my friends in school I'll definitely go clubbing cus I have crazy friends . I don't do drugs, I don't smoke ,and I take my academics seriously, which is quite unusual for guys like me. In school, I get the girls I want ,not because my parents are rich, no , I dress moderately, and I don't take my car to school , except on rare occasions. Mind you, I have a red BENZ AmG 2020 convertible, a very beautiful car that any teen would really love, but my friends drive it around the most, and I only take it for rides whenever I'm too tired to walk or whenever I'm going to a party. Well, basically, my life in school is just party club school and ladies.

I had left my mom's place in NY, and I was enjoying my second year of college in the lovely state of Massachusetts. I had a lovely sorority girlfriend and my grades were performing fine as usual, however something was lacking in my life. What was it you ask? Notches on my belt!

I was living in my modest but wonderfully equipped apartment. Pussy was simple as always . And I haven't lost my charm.

Sometimes during my leisure time, I went to the Martial Arts Club on campus to utilise the bags for a free exercise. Most of them geeky jerks utilised the club to practice maneuvers they saw in Jackie Chan movies. I utilized the time to practice boxing and Muay Thai techniques I acquired from a buddy who had a brother in the military helped keep me in condition. One of the evenings I was there, I saw a stunning female practicing high kicks like they might really work in a fight. Her technique wasn't horrible but her jiggling tits were fantastic. Cute pink shorts complemented her tanned legs well as she whirled for another outrageous dance. She made karate sexy. Each punch showed off a little of her toned belly while each kick left my imagination thinking what her thighs would look like wrapped around my head.

Any notion of working out fled my thoughts as she leaped to a new position. A tempting pair of tits trembled trying to keep up with each movement. Her absence of a sports bra was clear to even the shortest of looks.

As soon as her terrible karate act was complete, I introduced myself in hopes of ploughing her pussy. She offered me a warm grin as soon as I introduced myself.

"I know who you are; I've met a couple of your pals," she added with a grin. "I'm Amanda."

"Who have you met?" I inquired suspiciously.

"Some of your fraternity guys," Amanda said.

"Don't trust all they may have said about me," I said jokingly.

Her girlish chuckle made me think how simple it would be to openly flirt. Some females strive to seem clever and avoid flirting. Fortunately, Amanda wasn't one of those snotty sorts.

"Would you want to go grab something to eat?" I asked her to pack up her training stuff.

"Eww, I can't. I'm too sweaty to be in public," she said with a pouty grimace.

"Well then it was good meeting you," I casually added hoping she would accept the bait.

"We could tomorrow if you like!" Amanda said immediately.

"Okay, what's your number?"

She accepted my phone when I gave it then entered her name and number as quickly as her small fingers could go.

After our talk, I walked back to my fraternity home and fucked my girlfriend while secretly thinking about Amanda's swinging tits and tanned legs.

The following several days passed with little more than a few messages and nice words about wanting to meet for lunch. Truthfully, we were both too occupied with college. It took about a week before we met one other again face to face.

We arranged to meet at a Chinese restaurant near our college that was widely known for pricey tequila and wonderful noodles. She proposed and I consented, as I wanted to make a first time impression.

When she stepped through the door, I was struck breathless again by her beauty. A short black skirt danced with each high heel step, but her tight pink tee top is what caught my attention. It was draped over her breasts making her lovely C cups stand out like delectable double D's.

Lunch passed by in a whirl of flirty comments and cold margaritas. All of my charm was placed upon the table that day and it had the impact any guy could want. After two hours, she was inebriated and quietly indicating I should transport her back to her flat. I picked up on the signs after the first time she bit her lip and gazed into my eyes, but I continued playing hard to get until she began making allusions to her dick sucking talents. What a foolish harlot! Just my sort of chick!

I paid the check then walked Amanda to my '2020 AmG convertible, and let her fall into the passenger seat. I knew I was a bit too intoxicated to be driving, but I didn't care. Pussy was more significant than a DUI threat.

Happily, we made it back to her place in one piece owing to some one eye open driving on my side. It took longer for her to get her key into the door than it did for me to get mine into the ignition.

I had a roommate, not because I couldn't afford the rent alone, but because I wanted someone around to converse with so I don't lose my sanity to boredom. I screamed out

"James", and the entire house was silent, "My roommate is probably in class, cus he informed me he'll be studying late today. So we have the home all to ourselves." Amanda replied with a mischievous smirk as we staggered drunkenly into her flat.

"Great, where is your room?" I inquired hungrily.

"This way," she responded.

We stormed into her room like a sex bomb. Clothes flew rapidly as our hands explored one others' bodies. She drunkenly threw me back into the bed and my fingers began to push her underwear to one side.

"Oh wait!" Amanda said unexpectedly. "I can't."

"Why not?"

"I'm on my menstruation," she remarked regretfully. "But I can get you off now, okay?"

I shrugged, "okay."

She went down on me. Sadly, her blowjob was underwhelming. I certainly wasn't impressed. Maybe it was the drink or her attitude, but I wasn't enjoying it at all. She ended after an eternity of sucking and I felt bored and barely fulfilled.

I departed as soon as I could find an excuse with the pledge of never coming after her again. That was a mistake. I should have done the job as soon as she stopped bleeding.

A year had gone since the last time I saw Amanda. She had contacted me incessantly for a month following our initial meeting, but her poor dick sucking abilities left me disappointed. Basically, I didn't believe she was worth my time, I had more gorgeous fishes to fry.

Her name was nearly totally obliterated from my consciousness until she wrote to me on Facebook one frigid November night. I was engaged perusing the net when messager delivered a notice, I opened it and saw;

"Hey jack, how ya been? I realize we've not had the opportunity to chat in a while. Me and my boyfriend were looking for another guy for a threesome. I was informed you got kinky. I recall your pleasure. Get in touch with me if you are interested! K bye!"

The prospect of ploughing her left me fascinated. I spent a solid five minutes considering if she was worth the cracked nut or not. The only reason I ultimately consented was because I knew my closest buddy would trash me repeatedly if I turned down his new number so easily. My closest buddy and roommate James also really wanted to screw Amanda but think it will forever be a dream cus, he's like the reverse of me, he doesn't have a muscular physique, he doesn't have a vehicle, and he is less of a Playboy.

She provided me with her phone number on Facebook then I phoned her later that day.

"Hey Amanda, how have you been?" I inquired as soon as she said hi.

"Busy with work and school," she remarked, sighing; "how about you?"

"Same," I said.

"Why didn't you ever call me back the last time we went out?" Amanda asked sincerely.

"Sorry, I was terribly busy," I lied.

"That's what I figured. So are you interested in my message?"

"Very," I said with a grin.

"I may have to get drunk for this to work," Amanda joked into the phone.

"Then I'll bring some beverages," I said cheerfully.

"Okay, I relocated since the last time we chatted. I'll text you my address. You may come over at 10 if you like," she stated with a business tone.

"Okay, I'll call before I come over."

"Talk to you then," Amanda stated before hanging up.

Every idea I had for the remainder of the day blended with memories of her gorgeous tits. Classes appeared to drag on, and every interaction seemed to be uttered through a haze. My mind always focuses exclusively on what's vital. That day, nothing was more essential than Amanda's pussy.

Each hour felt like an eternity, even though each minute went like a second. Time has a way of messing with a horny man's brain, right?

Anyways, school completed at four and I spent many hours sipping beers with my fraternity guys before phoning her again.

"Hey, my boyfriend is getting off work soon if you want to come over," Amanda replied after we chatted for a few minutes on the phone. "I need to put on some clothing first. I just finished a shower."

"Don't bother about clothing. It would be hot if you answered the door nude."

"We'll see," she said with a smile.

We hung up after a few more suggestive comments. My raging hard-on was asking for the action, and I was ready to gratify my penis by ploughing her pussy. My objective was to fuck her so fantastically that she wanted to desert her partner for another night with me. What can I say, I'm a homewrecker!

I went to the supermarket and purchased a case of beer and some beef jerky so I would have something to eat when I left her home. (Planning ahead is what tiggers do best, bitch!)

After getting the necessary ingredients for a good night, I drove to a house near campus. She had leased the upper level as a loft apartment. I was obliged to park on the side of the small town road since there wasn't enough room in the drive-way. The area was pleasant so I didn't mind. Besides, my head was elsewhere as I enthusiastically ran up the outer set of steps. She opened the door in a little bathrobe and a grin after I had been banging for a full minute.

"Hey, come in," Amanda said, opening the door for me.

I stepped inside clutching a case of cheap Natty Light as she locked the door behind me. Her lovely physique had only become better with time. Her tanned legs seemed stronger, her butt looked even more toned, and her large tits looked as perky as before. What drew my attention this time however was how much her face had altered. Before she had light brown hair, but now platinum blonde hair complimented her facial features nicely. Her lovely brown eyes seemed brighter, her eyelashes looked longer, and her scarlet lips looked bigger. It was the first time I discovered how much hair style can influence everything you notice about a girl's face. She had preserved the same girlish expression as I observed her unhidden beauty.

"Am I different from you?" Amanda inquired as I attempted to mask my astonished face.

"Yeah, your hair looks wonderful," I responded, attempting to regain my wits.

"Thanks, I just got it done last week," she responded, running her fingers through it. "Do you actually enjoy it or are you simply saying that?"

"I believe that suits you great," I replied, coming closer to her.

"I'm pleased you enjoy it," she answered placing her hands upon my chest. "You really should have phoned me."

She chewed her lip staring up at me like I should apologise for being a jerk. Too bad, I never apologies to sluts.

"What are you wearing beneath this?" I requested untying the belt on her robe. She leaned back as I pulled the knot loose. Her satin robe slid open as the knot broke way. Her breasts came into view as she continued to bite her lip. The expression in her eyes was one urgently seeking acceptance.

"You are so lovely," I muttered before kissing her lightly.

Amanda's whimper against my lips was enough of a reaction for me to know she wanted more. We wrapped our arms around one other as we tumbled playfully into the sofa. Our tongues caressed as my hands glided over her toned young body. Her legs curled around my hips drawing us closer together. Her right breast heaved in my fingers as my finger tips slipped over her pink nipple. Another minute passed before we paused long enough to breathe.

"Oh yeah, I believe I need a drink after that," Amanda murmured, pushing softly on my chest so I would move off of her.

"I have beer if you want one," I remarked, staring at the case laying on the wooden floor.

"I detest beer," she remarked, pushing her hair back with manicured fingers. "I guess I have some tequila in my kitchen."

Amanda gave me another short kiss then led the way across her little loft apartment to a small kitchen. My eyes left her exquisite physique long enough to take in the little college apartment. The walls were barren save for an occasion poster or image. The wooden flooring proved the real antiquity of the property, but the reconstructed kitchenette made it evident the upper level hadn't been leased out for long. I stopped up looking at any more of the apartment as soon as she took a bottle of tequila off the counter and poured two party-sized shots.

"What time will your guy be here?" I asked taking the whole shot glass from her extended hand.

She shrugged; "he should be here shortly."

I took the shot and gave her back the glass. She turned her back to me and took the shot. It was a few seconds before I could see her face again.

"Why did you turn away?" I asked with a smirk.

"I make stupid expressions when I drink hard things," she said with a pouty look.

I giggled; "that's adorable."

"No it's not," she cried, stamping her feet like a small kid. Her tits jiggled in response and left my eyes following them hypnotically. She saw my attention and moved her hips a bit so her tits would keep moving.

"You like them don't you?" Amanda asked, grasping them gently.

"Yes," I responded, watching her squeeze her nipples.

A unexpected tap on the door jolted me back to reality.

"He's here!" Amanda yelled as she ran to the door.

I poured myself another shot of tequila in readiness to meet the bitch who was going to let me fuck his girlfriend.

Amanda stepped back into the kitchen followed by a shorter, very average-looking gentleman. He wasn't obese, didn't have muscles, and didn't even have great clothing. He was normal in every sense. I attempted to figure out how he landed Amanda, but I spared myself the idea by taking the tequila shot instead.

"Hi, great to meet you, I'm peter."

I shook his hand, "Nice to meet you too. Want a shot?"

I purposefully didn't give him my name when I gave Amanda's booze to the stranger.

"Yeah, let's all take shots!" Amanda cheered, grabbed her glass and another for peter.

We took two more shots while keeping the polite conversation flowing. He discussed where he worked and she spoke about education. I wasn't listening since I was too busy gazing at her tits which were still blatantly on exhibit. He scarcely glanced at her. He appeared to focus on the tequila pouring more. Finally, I became weary of the polite chat and inquired what her bedroom looked like.

"Oh, I can show you!" Amanda remarked, pushing my hand towards a locked door on the opposite side of her little loft apartment.

She unlocked the solid wooden door and turned the light switch quickly lighting her little bedroom.

"Don't mind the mess," she replied shoving some soiled garments aside from her queen sized bed. I peeked over her soiled clothing and unkempt bed to a cage next to her open wardrobe.

"What's that?" I inquired.

"That's my little weasel," Amanda shouted, gleefully hopping to the cage like a young girl on Christmas. She unlocked the cage door and brought out a live weasel.

"Why the Hell do you have a pet weasel?" I asked.

Peter laughed behind me. Apparently he agreed with my question.

She gave us a filthy look as she said; "I adore Monopoly." She embraced the weasel to convey her sentiments.

"You have a pet weasel called Monopoly?"

"Yes, don't make fun of him," she murmured, cuddling him closer.

"Whatever," I muttered, shaking my head. "Put him away and come over here."

I had bigger things to worry about than of a silly pet with a lousy name. Amanda closed the door with the weasel securely inside and slid up onto the bed. Her satin robe hung open as her tits swung back and forth.

"Why don't you two start," suggested Peter, withdrawing back to the bedroom door.

"Good idea," Amanda remarked, letting the robe fall off of her shoulders seductively.

I pulled off my black tee shirt and shoes as she proceeded to crawl over the bed to where I was standing. I stopped moving as she unfastened my belt and unbuttoned my blue pants. Her ass moved behind her as her lips brushed my lower abs. The remainder of my garments ended up on the floor as her right palm cupped my balls. She grabbed my hips hard making me fall into the bed. I nearly fell on her but I was able to adjust my weight at the last second.

Amanda giggled, "I think I'm a little tipsy."

"You're strong when you drink," I said, moving fully onto the bed.

She giggled again as she kissed my cock. Her manicured nails scratched lightly down my chest and abs while she kept kissing and licking my hard shaft. She paused once to wiggle her ass in Peter's direction, but his uneasy demeanor showed his reasons for keeping close to the door. She turned back to me and smiled.

"Guess it's just us for a few minutes."

Amanda accentuated her words by taking me all the way into her mouth. The slow sliding action of her tongue and lips made my eyes roll back into her head. This definitely wasn't the same blowjob as before. Her fingers slid up and down following the movements of her lips. Her tongue drove into me as her fingers twisted to match the powerful feelings. My thoughts shouted in excitement at her incredible new discovered skills.

"Do you want to fuck me?" Amanda questioned, staring up into my eyes a few minutes later.

"Yes," I answered breathlessly.

"Peter, could you buy us a couple condoms," she asked without glancing away from me.

I looked at him long enough to see him do what he was instructed. She sat up and accepted one as he held them out for her.

"You should take off your clothes too," she replied glancing at him.

He pulled off his clothing but kept a ways back from the bed. He continued tugging at his flaccid dick as Amanda gazed at him sympathetically.

"I'm a bit nervous," he added nervously.

Amanda shook her head and unwrapped the condom packet. I lay back and let her put it on. She chuckled and delighted as she slid the tight rubber down. I'm not hung but the little condoms made my dick feel like it was being shrink wrapped. I could hardly feel her pussy as she sank her hips onto my waiting dick.

She grinded back and forth as I attempted to restore sensation; "is anything wrong?" She inquired after noticing the painful expression on my face.

"These condoms suck. They are too little," I said.

"Sorry," Peter murmured regretfully.

Amanda proceeded to flex her hips like a porn star. I clutched her breasts trying to keep my mind off of the agony growing on my cock. Finally, I shoved her off of me and got up.

"Peter, you should have a turn bro," I shouted, irritated at the condom.

Amanda stroked her pussy while gazing at me. "What's wrong?"

"This condom is hurting me," I answered.

Peter sat on the bed next to her and caressed her pussy while his other hand furiously grasped his flaccid man meat. I fled the room pulling off the miserable rubber. It was the first time I had ever been too large for a condom. It should have made me feel masculine, but it left me irritated instead. I strolled into the kitchen and put the condom into the kitchen sink with a smirk then poured myself another shot. I assumed she could clean up after me if she wasn't going to get me off. I could hear hushed murmurs coming from the bedroom, but I didn't care what they were saying.

"Pour me one too," Amanda remarked exiting the bedroom a few minutes later.

"Why aren't you in there having sex with peter? I was coming back," I added, refilling her shot glass.

"He can't stay hard," she stated with a groan.

"Well it occurs."

"It hasn't happened to you," she murmured, turning away from me to sip the booze.

"Yeah, well, you're hot," I said while studying her butt when she took the shot. She turned back around a few seconds later with a grin.

"You're sweet," Amanda murmured, laying the glass on the counter and sinking on her knees in front of me.

She took my dick back into her mouth with renewed energy. I leaned back against the counter and closed my eyes while she worked. Peter came out of the bedroom and sat on the couch looking defeated while his girlfriend sucked my growing dick enthusiastically. Seems he was also startled since my dick was that large with veins, big enough to be someone else's dick , I smiled and thought to myself.

"Let's go back to the bedroom," I murmured with a ravenous expression in my eyes.

Determination to make her scream directed my thoughts as she rose up and grabbed my hand guiding me back to the bedroom. Peter followed us like a sad puppy. Amanda got onto the bed and wiggled her ass as Peter gave me another condom. I slipped it on violently and entered her from behind. Her sudden intake of breath was enough to tell me she loved doggy style.

Another moan escaped her lips before she bit the pillow to hide the sounds. I pulled her hair thrusting into her again. Her face lifted from the pillow as I pulled harder and another loud moan echoed in the bedroom. Each thrust was met by another moan, and they started to come faster and louder as I sped up. My dick hurt from the rubber, but I didn't care. The groans felt like encouragement and my instincts reacted. I pushed deeper and faster and the condom stretched further and further. I pushed in hard enough to start bunching the rubber at the bottom of my dick. The condom continued expanding as I kept fucking her. Her pussy got wetter and my dick sank deeper and deeper. Her groans got more animalistic and she stated she was going to come. I drove in again and felt the condom break beneath our desperate motions. Instantly, wave after wave of ecstasy overwhelmed my senses. Her hot tight pussy seized my naked cock. It was great! She must have felt it snap too because she grinded her hips back into mine.

"Don't stop," she yelled. "I'm cumming!"

She attempted to hide her face into the cushion, but my palm grabbed her hair too firmly. The moans rang loudly enough to wake up everybody within a block of her upper flat. After the first orgasm, she turned over and pleaded for another. I responded her by thrusting my naked cock into her and maintaining my furious pace. I paused barely long enough to pull the damaged rubber off. She observed me and grinned. peter probably wanted to say anything but he was too much of a bitch to make a sound as I raped his girlfriend. Finally, after a full hour of vigorous sex and multiple heart stopping orgasms, she recommended we take a break.

"I'm going to be hurting tomorrow," Amanda muttered, attempting to catch her breath.

We tumbled onto the bed in a hot ball of passion and wasted energy. Peter sat on the floor nude and forgotten. After a few minutes of resting, I checked the time on my phone and proceeded to get ready.

"Call me if you want to do this again," I added, zipping up my pants.

"You're leaving? You haven't cummed yet," she remarked regretfully.

"That's alright, you can simply make me cum tomorrow," I said pulling on my shirt.

"Okay, I'll call you after class," she responded, drawing a blanket over her nude body.

I walked over Peter's legs and left the flat without even saying good-bye to him. Once I hopped into my vehicle, I opened the bag of beef jerky and switched on my engine. It was certainly a wonderful night for Amanda and myself. It was probably a horrible night for Peter, but he's a little bitch and no one cares what he thinks.

The craziest aspect of the tale is that I believe they two ended up getting married.

www.ingramcontent.com/pod-product-compliance
Lightning Source LLC
Chambersburg PA
CBHW061531120726
48001CB00004B/1490